The Little One

The Little One

by Florence Heide

illustrated by Ken Longtemps

THE LION PRESS

Publishers, New York

Copyright © 1970 by The Lion Press, Inc.
21 West 38th Street, New York, N.Y. 10018
All rights reserved
Published simultaneously in Canada by George J. McLeod Ltd.
73 Bathurst Street, Toronto 2B, Ontario
Library of Congress Catalog Card Number 70-112647
ISBN: 0-87460-071-5; Libr. Ed: 0-87460-138-X
This book was printed and bound in the United States of America

100224

The Little One walked alone.

He came to a sea gull.
"I have wings, and I can fly," said the sea gull.
"I have no wings," said the Little One.

The Little One walked on.
He came to a horse.
"I can run like the wind," said the horse.

"I cannot," said the Little One.

The Little One walked on.
He came to a fish.
"I can swim to the bottom of the sea if I like," said the fish.
"I cannot," said the Little One.

The Little One walked on.
He came to a cat.
"I can see in the dark," said the cat.
"I cannot," said the Little One.

The Little One walked on.
He came to a mole.
"I can build tunnels under the ground,"
    said the mole.
"I cannot," said the Little One.

The Little One walked on.
He came to an elephant.
"I am as strong as a dozen men," said the elephant.
"I am not strong," said the Little One.

The Little One walked on.
"What can I do?" he wondered.
"What can I do that the sea gull can't do, or the horse,
or the fish, or the cat, or the mole, or the elephant?"

The Little One walked on.
He came to a door.

"I can open this door," said the Little One.
"I cannot," said the sea gull.
"I cannot," said the horse.
"I cannot," said the fish.
"I cannot," said the cat.
"I cannot," said the mole.
"I cannot," said the elephant.
"I can open this door," said the Little One,
    opening it. "And I can climb these stairs.

"I can learn to think
            and plan
                and dream
                    and do
"I can learn to be a man!
"And when I am a man—
"I can learn to make things and build things . . .

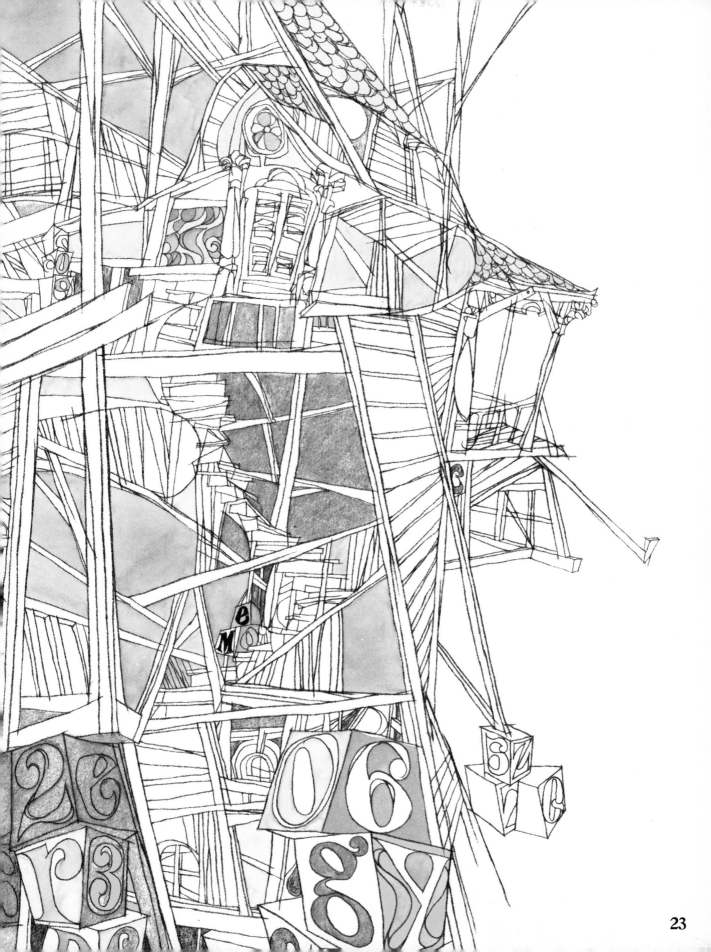

"I can build something that will take me as fast
as the wind,

"I can build something that will carry me through
the skies.

and something that will take me deep in the sea.

"I can build something that will let me
    see in the dark,
and something that will help me
    dig down, down, deep into the ground.

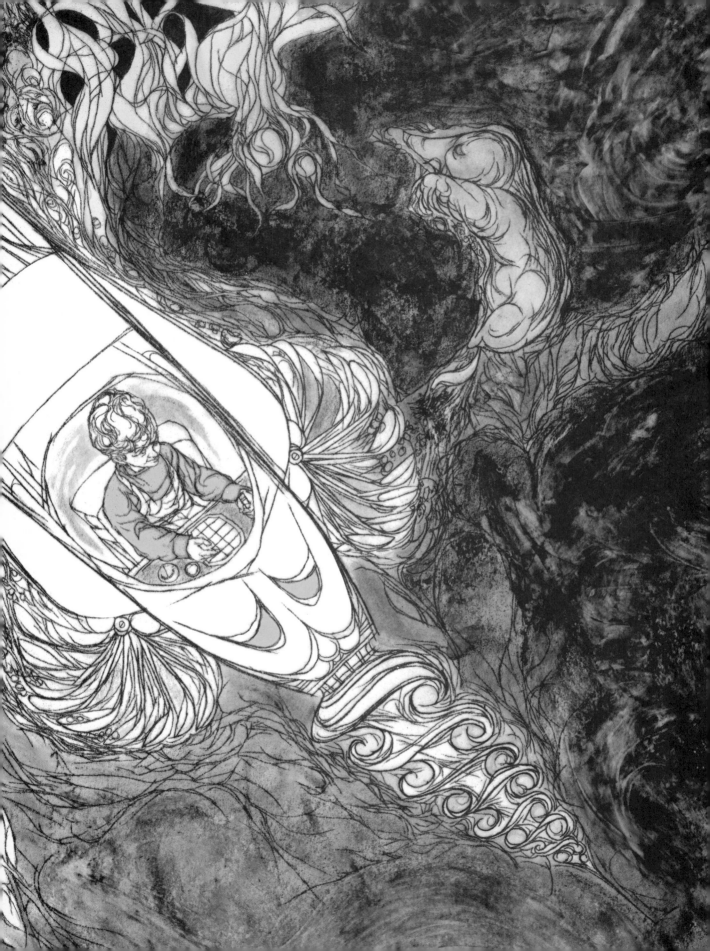

"And I can build something strong enough to help me
tear down buildings to make room for new ones.
I can build bridges, or move mountains!
And things no man has dreamed of yet, I can do
when I'm a man," said the Little One.

And he did.